P9-DGR-327

FAREWELL, AUNT ISABELL

FAREWELL, AUNT ISABELL

by

ILSE-MARGRET VOGEL

Pictures by the Author

Harper & Row, Publishers
New York, Hagerstown, San Francisco, London

Farewell, Aunt Isabell

Printed in the United States of America. For information address Harper & Row, Publishers, Inc., 10 East 53rd Street, New York, N.Y. 10022. Published simultaneously in Canada by Fitzhenry & Whiteside Limited, Toronto.
FIRST EDITION

Library of Congress Cataloging in Publication Data
Vogel, Ilse-Margret.
Farewell, Aunt Isabell.

SUMMARY: Two young sisters try to make their mentally ill aunt happy so that she will get well.
[1. Mentally ill–Fiction] I. Title.
PZ7.V867Far [Fic] 79-1785
ISBN 0-06-026317-2
ISBN 0-06-026318-0 lib. bdg.

For you, Tante Hilde,
who still share
some of my memories.

CONTENTS

FAREWELL, AUNT ISABELL

Chapter One

"You go in first," Erika said, stepping behind me.

"No," I said, "you go."

Erika shook her head and shoved me toward the door.

"No, no, no—*you* go first," I insisted. "You are older than I."

We stood before the door of Aunt Isabell's room. Only an hour ago Grandmother, Mother and a nurse we had never seen before had climbed out of a large hospital car with barred windows. Behind them stood Aunt Isabell. It seemed she did not want to leave the car. Dodo, our grandmother, had to coax her out. Finally Aunt Isabell stepped down and was led along the garden path into the house and up to her room. A short time later Mother came to our room. "Go up now and greet Aunt Isabell," she told us.

We were dying to see Aunt Isabell again ever since we had been told she would be coming home soon. We had been terribly curious when workmen came to install iron grates over two big windows on the second floor of our house. "Is she well again?" Erika had asked. The answer was a sad smile. "Not really," Dodo had said, "but we *must* get her out of that terrible place. In such hospitals life is unbearable." Dodo's eyes had filled with tears as they always did when she and Mother returned from their weekly visits to Aunt Isabell.

* * *

Now she was home and we were at her door to greet her.

"All right," Erika said, "I'll knock and we both will enter together and—"

"And hold hands," I added.

And that's what we did. We entered, closed the door behind us and pressed our backs against it. There stood Aunt Isabell between Dodo and Nurse Amelia.

"Hello. How are you?" we said in unison. We made a little curtsy, but did not cross the room to throw our arms around Aunt Isabell's neck as we used to do a year ago. There was something about her that held us back.

Aunt Isabell did not say a word.

"Hello," we said again. "How are you?"

No response. Aunt Isabell looked us over from head to toe. We stood still and looked back. She had not changed much during the year we had not seen her. Thinner, yes, much thinner, and without a smile. Our backs were still pressed against the door, and in desperation, not knowing what else to do, I asked for the third time, "How are you?"

This time Aunt Isabell answered. "Fine," she said, "but why are your shoes shit-yellow?"

I felt my face get hot. Never had I heard our parents, grandparents, uncles or aunts use that word. When occasionally Erika or I said it, we got a scolding or even a slap on the shoulder.

I looked down at Erika's and my shoes. They were the same nice brownish yellow, still shining with newness. We were speechless.

"Shit-yellow," Aunt Isabell repeated. "Why?"

Dodo walked over to us, opened the door and said, "You can leave now, darlings."

We were out of the room fast, but stood rooted to the floor. We could hear Dodo's voice behind the closed door. Tenderly and slowly she said, "Isabell, you always liked Erika and Inge. Don't you anymore?"

"No! No! No!" Isabell screamed and, raising her voice even more, she added, "I LOVE them!"

This outburst made Erika and me run downstairs and through the garden until we came to the small brook at the end of our property. Breathless, we sat down. For a long time we did not say a word.

Erika broke the silence. "Did you imagine she would be like *that*?" she asked.

"And do you want to be loved like *that*?" I answered.

We both fell silent again. We just sat there shaking our heads.

* * *

A few hours later we all sat around the supper table. Aunt Isabell and Nurse Amelia, however, remained upstairs.

"Dodo," I asked, "is Aunt Isabell *really* well now?"

There was a silence. I saw Dodo and Mother exchange glances.

Then Dodo said, "Well—she is *nearly* well."

And Mother added, "You need not be afraid of Aunt Isabell. We will see to it that she is completely well soon."

"How?" Erika wanted to know.

And Dodo, her voice full of hope, explained, "We all will give her love and care. The good food, the healthy country air and the helping nurse will do the rest."

"Yes, yes," Mother interrupted, "all this will mean a fast recovery for Aunt Isabell."

"And tomorrow we will let Aunt Isabell see Roland. That will make her happy," Dodo said.

Roland was our big, beautiful shepherd dog. He really belonged to Aunt Isabell, but during the long year of her absence Erika and I had come to think of him as our dog. And, to be honest, I felt Roland was *my* dog. Erika did not like this idea, but Roland followed me around most of the day. And often he slept at the end of my bed all night. Even Erika had to admit that.

"Do I have to share Roland with Aunt Isabell?" I asked Dodo before going to bed.

Dodo looked at me with astonishment. "But darling, I am sure you *want* to do anything that might make Aunt Isabell happy. Everything that makes her happy will also make her well faster."

"Oh, yes," I said, "I do." And I meant it.

* * *

Next morning Dodo asked me to put Roland on a leash and come upstairs with her to see Aunt Isabell.

"Dodo," I said, "Roland is never on a leash. He will not like it."

Dodo insisted. Roland growled a bit, tried to shake himself loose, but quieted down when I stroked him.

Dodo entered Aunt Isabell's room first to tell her I was bringing Roland. As soon as I was inside, Roland tore himself loose. Barking, he jumped on Aunt Isabell, putting his front paws on her shoulders.

Aunt Isabell screamed. The nurse screamed. Finally I screamed, too, calling Roland back. It was Dodo who separated the dog and Aunt Isabell. I grabbed his collar and pulled him out of the room. He quieted down immediately and started to lick my face.

"Roland," I said, "Roland. We wanted to make Aunt Isabell happy. Why did you startle her so much?"

But Roland just kept licking my face as if nothing had happened.

Chapter Two

Three days passed without Erika or me seeing Aunt Isabell. We often looked up to the iron-grated windows. Once or twice we thought we saw Aunt Isabell and we waved. The vague figure withdrew immediately.

Dodo and Nurse Amelia took turns staying with Aunt Isabell. She was never left alone and the door was locked with a key—at all times.

The talks at mealtime were always about Aunt Isabell. How she had slept, how much she had eaten, what she had said. Had she smiled or had she, as she often did, been sitting on the edge of her bed staring at the ceiling? "Thank God, how much better she is already," Mother would say. And Dodo would nod agreement.

Father did not say much. How could he? He was never home during the day. He left the house early in the morning, walked five minutes to the railroad station and took a train that brought him to the city half an hour later. In the early evening Erika and I would often go to the station to wait for Father's train. Sometimes we would go earlier, to see the big express trains whizz by our station, waving all the time as if the whole train was full of friends.

So, at the dinner table, Father would just listen to the Aunt Isabell tale. Once in a while he asked a question, but mainly he kept quiet.

Erika and I missed his talks, his telling us about his work. Father was a lawyer, a divorce lawyer, but most of the time he worked hard to get couples together again. There were often funny stories which made us all laugh. But now there was not time for that. We tried to understand. Thinking and talking about how to make Aunt Isabell well again were more important.

"She needs to feel loved," Mother, who was Aunt Isabell's sister, said over and over again.

"Yes, happy and loved," Dodo always added.

*   *   *

The next day was the first real summer day. Dew fresh was the morning, but it got warm very fast.

"Let's go to the brook," Erika suggested after lunch. "I bet the meadow is full of marguerites."

The end of our large garden bordered on a brook. It was shallow but swiftly flowing. Willows and bushes followed its meandering course. We loved to splash in it, pick its smooth pebbles, watch frogs jump in and out and see water bugs skate over the surface.

As soon as we reached the brook we took off our sandals, pushed our way through the low, thick bushes and started wading downstream. Erika went ahead.

"Slower, slower," I told her. "There's so much to see." But she hurried on. I discovered a whole cluster of tiny frogs sunning themselves on a flat stone. "Come back, Erika," I called. "You missed something great."

Instead of answering, Erika screamed, "You come!" she shouted. "Come *fast*!"

When I reached her side I, too, let out a scream. There before us lay Aunt Isabell, the sparkling water running over her whole body. Her hands were folded on her chest as if in prayer. Her water-blue eyes stared up to the sky and strands of her brown hair were floating next to her pale, thin face. She had a wreath of flowers on her head. A pretty wreath of marguerites, forget-me-nots and yellow buttercups.

We were paralyzed. I don't know how long we stood and stared. I started to weep first.

"She looks so pretty dead," Erika sobbed. I nodded and wiped my nose on my sleeve. Erika took out a handkerchief and dried my tears.

At that moment we heard loud laughter. We looked up and saw Aunt Isabell sitting up in the brook. She was shaking with laughter.

"You thought I was dead," she said triumphantly. "You *really* thought I was dead."

Then she was on her feet. She reached for our hands and pulled us through the bushes to the open meadow. She was dripping all over, but the sun shone warm and she didn't seem to mind.

"Beautiful," she said. "Isn't this meadow beautiful?" Without waiting for an answer she continued, "Now we will make a wreath for each of you. Do you know how? Oh, you don't? Well, I'll show you. First you pick the flowers. Go on! Let the stems be as long as possible. All colors! We want as many colors as possible. Yes, that's fine. Now look—"

She sat down in the tall grass and started to twist the flower stems in a special way. Then she took my hands and guided them in the same manner. Soon the chain of flowers was long enough to go around my head and Aunt Isabell closed it to make a circle. She put it on my head and kissed me. "Darling Inge," she whispered, "you have grown so much and you are so pretty."

Then she made a wreath for Erika, put it on her head and kissed her too.

It was all fun and nice now, although we really hadn't quite gotten over our shock yet. Aunt Isabell must have felt that.

"Come on," she said. "Let's be gay now. You know I myself was very sad only an hour ago because *how* can I ever find a bridegroom being locked up in that prison room upstairs? But I managed to slip out, come to the meadow and make myself a wreath of flowers. Then I waited for my bridegroom to arrive. He didn't show up. That's why I put myself in the murmuring brook. Now I'm married to him. Come, let's have a wedding dance!"

We linked hands and started to dance. Aunt Isabell was singing a song about bringing someone a bridal wreath made out of marguerites, forget-me-nots, a ribbon of sky-blue silk and hope. She

sang it over and over and we kept on dancing and dancing. Finally we got dizzy and let ourselves fall into the high grass. The grass was so tall it closed in over our heads forming arches. We could see many different kinds of little bugs climbing up and down the blades. We heard the humming and buzzing of bees flying from clover to clover. The whole meadow was alive. Then little bugs started crawling over us. We brushed them off gently, but when a pretty ladybug struggled up my arm, I picked it up carefully and put it on Aunt Isabell's arm. She laughed, picked it up and put it on Erika's knee. We all giggled and laughed and were happy.

* * *

Suddenly we heard voices. Urgent voices calling, "Isabell! Isabell! Where are you, Isabell?"

Aunt Isabell put her finger to her lips. "Hush," she whispered. "Don't answer. They won't find us. The three of us are so happy here."

The voices came closer and closer. Now we could distinguish between Mother's and Nurse Amelia's voice. We could hear the worry and the anguish. But what were we to do? Being happy will make Aunt Isabell well faster, we remembered. So we kept quiet until the voices faded in the distance.

Aunt Isabell stood up and straightened her dress.

It was nearly dry now. "We will go for a walk," she declared.

"Hadn't we better go home?" Erika asked.

"No," Aunt Isabell said with great determination, "we will go for a walk."

Erika and I looked at each other. It did not feel quite right to let them all worry so much at home, but on the other hand Aunt Isabell's happiness seemed more important.

Aunt Isabell took our hands and started walking.

"If we follow the brook, we come to a road," she said, "and if we follow the road, we soon will be at the railroad station. That's where I want to go."

And we did. At the station we stood at the iron fence separating the small station building with its ticket window from the tracks. We leaned our elbows on the fence. Erika and I had to climb a few rungs to be able to do this. While we waited for the trains to come, we stretched our necks and turned our heads to be able to see them approach from far away.

Aunt Isabell talked. She talked happily and without stopping. "You know, darlings, one day I shall go to Greece and see all the beautiful temples in Athens."

We looked at her in surprise. "Isn't that far

away?" Erika asked.

Aunt Isabell paid no attention. "Of course, I will take both of you with me," she went on. "You will love it! The white marble temples, the colorfully painted fishing boats on the blue Aegean Sea. Then we will go to—"

The roar of a train rushing by swallowed Aunt Isabell's words.

"—then we will go to Egypt," she continued, "to see the pyramids and the sphinxes rising out of the yellow sand, drenched in sunlight. The Nile will be full of crocodiles, of course, but you need not be afraid. I will always protect you. I have fought worse monsters. Believe me! The hospital I was in was *full* of them! And if you want, we can —"

The next train was catching our attention and washing out her words. It, too, rushed past and Aunt Isabell went on.

"We can sail down the Nile and go deep into black Africa. There jungles and monkeys will wait for us. The black people don't have black souls, believe me! The blackest souls I ever found I found in white people. I know what I'm talking about."

Now Erika interrupted. "But how will we ever get there?" she asked.

"Don't worry," Aunt Isabell said. "Didn't I get you

to the beautiful meadow? Didn't I find the way to the railroad station?"

"Yes," Erika said, "but shouldn't we go home now?"

I pointed to the huge station clock. "Look, it's only five minutes till Father's train. Let's wait for him."

Aunt Isabell filled these five minutes with another trip. This time she promised to take us to France. We would go to Paris with all its museums and parks, with its gay cafés in the streets where people sit all night talking and laughing and drinking good wines.

She wasn't half through with our Paris trip when Father's train rolled into the station. I could see how surprised he was to see Aunt Isabell with us. But he didn't let on. He casually told us how uncomfortably hot it had been in town and how he was looking forward to a quiet evening on the lawn.

When we reached home, however, there was no quiet. Dodo, Mother and Nurse Amelia had cried their eyes red and were just giving information to two policemen whom they had summoned by telephone. Dodo was the first to collect herself when she saw us. She simply took Aunt Isabell's hand and led her to the stairs. Aunt Isabell's mood had changed abruptly when she saw the two men in uniform. Cursing and complaining loudly, she had to be pulled and shoved up the stairs.

Then Mother told us she had no real supper ready and hastily put bread, butter and cold cuts on the table.

Everybody was quiet, but Erika and I felt fine. In detail and frequently interrupting each other, we told what a wonderful afternoon we had had with Aunt Isabell dancing in the meadow.

"She was *so* happy," I ended our report. "You will see she will be well very soon."

Chapter Three

Several quiet days followed. We did not see Aunt Isabell although we heard the usual reports at mealtimes.

"What could we do today to make Aunt Isabell happy?" I asked Erika one rainy morning.

"I know," she answered. "We could make an apron for her. A very pretty apron."

We begged Dodo for a piece of cloth. She took us to her room. There stood the huge chest in which she stored hundreds of remnants. She raised the heavy oak lid. We knelt on the floor beside the chest and Dodo began fishing about through the wonderfully colored pieces of velvet and linen, of cotton and laces. This in itself was always a feast for us. Often she would stop and caress a piece of material.

"This comes from the skirt I wore when I met your grandfather for the first time," she told us. For a second she pressed the blue linen against her cheek. Then she put it back in the chest. "And this piece of red velvet is a leftover from the dresses I sewed for you to wear on Christmas day. You were three years old then and you, Inge, spilled a full cup of cocoa down your chest immediately."

"Was I scolded for being so clumsy?" I asked.

"No, no, you were not," Dodo said. "Quite the opposite. We had to comfort you because you were in tears about the big stain on your new dress."

And so it went on. Memories clinging to each bit of cloth grew into stories. We loved it and had almost forgotten what we were looking for until Dodo said, "Here–that's it. Just enough for an apron." She handed us a piece of fine gray linen.

"Gray?" I said, disappointed. "Just gray?"

But Erika immediately had an idea. "We will embroider it," she said. "We will make a wide, colorful border at the bottom."

"And on the pocket we will put Aunt Isabell's initials," I suggested.

Dodo gave us thread, needles and embroidery yarn. We went to work at once, but it took us three days to finish. First I made up the design on a piece of paper. Then we both started cross-stitching from opposite sides of the apron until a wide red-green-and-blue border was finished.

The moment we had done the last stitch we wanted to bring it to Aunt Isabell, but Dodo told us Aunt Isabell had had a bad night. She was not feeling well and so we would have to wait until tomorrow.

* * *

The next day Dodo took us upstairs. Aunt Isabell greeted us warmly.

"We have a present for you, Aunt Isabell," I said.

"Yes, we both made it," Erika explained. "Close your eyes, Aunt Isabell, until we tell you to open them."

She did and quickly we tied the apron around her waist. We pulled her out into the hall in front of a tall mirror.

"Now open your eyes," Erika said.

Aunt Isabell looked at the mirror.

"Who is that?" she asked, pointing at her reflection.

"Aunt Isabell, it's *you*!" I exclaimed.

Aunt Isabell shook her head, turned to Dodo and asked, "You tell me, *who* is that person?"

"You, Isabell. It is you."

"No," Aunt Isabell said, "no!" She covered her eyes with her hands.

"Certainly it's you," Dodo said. "Look at the pretty apron Erika and Inge have made for you."

Aunt Isabell did not take her hands from her eyes, but she must have peeked through her fingers because she said, "Yes, it is a pretty apron." She uncovered her eyes and used her hands to stroke the apron.

For a moment it looked as if Aunt Isabell would smile. But she didn't. Instead she frowned.

"There is only one thing wrong," she said severely, and she began to turn the apron on her body until it was covering her back and the tie bow was in front. "That way an apron makes more sense," she said. She smiled and thanked us.

We looked down at our own aprons. They were an important addition to the dirndl dresses we wore. The aprons were pretty and showy, more for decoration than protection.

"What about ours, Aunt Isabell?" I asked.

"Wrong. All wrong," she answered with great emphasis that was close to anger. Frightened, we began turning our aprons until they too covered the backs of our skirts.

Now Aunt Isabell laughed and laughed. We joined in her laughter.

"We have made her happy again," I whispered in Erika's ear.

But when Aunt Isabell did not stop laughing and we saw Dodo's worried face, we began to feel uncomfortable. Mother, who was downstairs, must have been roused by the laughter. She came to the foot of the stairs.

"What's this all about?" she called up.

"Oh, the apron. My beautiful apron," Aunt Isabell answered, interrupting her laughter for a moment. "Wait, I'll come down and show you."

And before any of us could do anything, Aunt Isabell began to descend the stairs backwards, so Mother would see the apron. After the first two steps she fell. She fell hard and rolled down half the stairs.

When we reached her, she was still laughing though blood from the back of her head trickled down her neck.

We were sent away while Mother and Nurse Amelia carried the laughing and struggling Aunt Isabell back upstairs.

We went to our room, but we could still hear the laughter. It went on and on without stopping. I couldn't stand it anymore. I grabbed Erika's arm.

"Let's go outside," I said, and Erika followed me willingly.

* * *

We went to the end of the garden, to the brook, but seeing it reminded me of finding Aunt Isabell lying in the water. Erika wanted to sit down. I resisted.

"No, not *here,*" I said.

Erika nodded; she understood. We went back to the garden and wandered about aimlessly until we were called to lunch.

Lunch was grim and quiet. Dodo stayed upstairs with Aunt Isabell. The moment Mother and Nurse Amelia had finished eating, they went upstairs too. We wanted to follow, but had been ordered to stay downstairs. Every so often we could still hear Aunt Isabell break out in laughter. By now it really frightened us.

"Let's go and tell Magda," Erika suggested.

Magda lived next door. Our garden bordered on hers. She was one year older than we were. When we were lucky–that is, when Maria, who lived on the other side of Magda's garden and who was a year older than Magda, did not play with her—Magda would play with us. Magda called us *the little ones.* We did not like this, but we would not have dared to criticize Magda.

Magda answered the doorbell.

"Are we bothering you?" I asked, seeing her sour-sweet smile.

"Well," she said, "Maria will be here soon and I have to braid my hair. What do you want, little ones? Is it something important?"

I nodded, but Erika said, "No. It can wait."

"It's about Aunt Isabell," I said hurriedly.

Mentioning Aunt Isabell, I had Magda's full attention at once.

"Go ahead, tell me," she said. "I can do my hair *and* listen."

So we told Magda how we had made the pretty apron for Aunt Isabell, had tied it around her waist and how she had turned it backwards, insisting that *that* was the proper way to wear an apron. We told it in every detail right up to Aunt Isabell's fall down the stairs. We told about the blood on her neck and then about her laughter.

"So?" Magda said. "Everything is fine. Your Aunt Isabell laughed. All's well that ends well." She started to laugh herself.

"But Aunt Isabell didn't stop laughing," Erika said meekly.

"So much the better," Magda said. "The more laughter, the happier Aunt Isabell was."

"You didn't *hear* that laughter," I interrupted. "It was scary."

"Nonsense," Magda declared. "You are too little and too dumb to understand. Laughter is laughter." Then, she suddenly put her arms around our shoulders and said, "Listen, I would like to see your Aunt Isabell. Can't you arrange that?"

We did not answer immediately.

"Come on," Magda urged, "you can do me that little favor." She kissed each of us on the cheek. "You see," she went on, "I have never seen a person who was in a crazy house. Now, what do you say?"

Erika and I looked at each other helplessly. I knew deep in my heart it was not right to give in to Magda's plea. But then she had put her arms around us and kissed us. We both nodded yes hesitantly.

"I'll come over with you right now," Magda said.

"No, not now," Erika said. "Besides, you said Maria was coming soon."

"Oh, Maria. She can wait. I would rather see your crazy aunt."

"That is not possible right now," I said firmly. "It must be arranged."

"All right," Magda said, giving in. "Tomorrow then."

Chapter Four

We spent all afternoon trying to figure out some way to keep our promise. Finally Erika had an idea.

"You remember how happy Aunt Isabell was dancing in the meadow?" she asked. "We can suggest going to the meadow again and Magda can hide in the bushes and watch."

"Will that work?" I asked.

"Certainly," Erika answered.

* * *

At breakfast next morning Dodo and Nurse Amelia, who had taken turns sleeping with Aunt Isabell, reported she had slept deeply all night through. She was calm, the wound on her head had almost healed and she was in good spirits.

That was when Erika suggested we should take Aunt Isabell to the meadow behind the brook again. Dodo and Mother shook their heads.

"But Aunt Isabell was so happy there," Erika insisted. "You should have *seen* how happy she was dancing with us."

"I can't see anything wrong with that," Nurse Amelia said. "I will go with them, of course, so they don't run off to the railroad station again. And since there is no road or even a footpath nearby, we won't meet anybody."

"All right," Dodo said, "but let's wait till after lunch."

That gave us time to tell Magda.

"You must stay in the bushes," Erika instructed her, "so you won't be seen."

"But I want to talk to your crazy aunt," Magda said.

"No, that is not possible," Erika said, "but you will be able to see her. That's what you asked for and that's what we promised you. To *see* her. But you must stay out of sight. Understand?"

Never had I heard Erika talk so sternly to Magda. I was surprised and I kept quiet.

*   *   *

When afternoon came, Aunt Isabell, Nurse Amelia and the two of us walked through the garden to the brook. Aunt Isabell looked with great interest at all the garden flowers, remembering many names, even the Latin ones.

"But," she said, "wild flowers out in the meadow are what I really like best. I'm so looking forward to seeing them again."

We reached the brook. Before crossing, Aunt Isabell bent down, cupped her hands, filled them with the clear water and raised them to her mouth.

"I must kiss my bridegroom," she said. She repeated this three times.

At that moment I thought I heard a giggle in the bushes nearby, but I did not turn my head.

Aunt Isabell crossed the brook. We followed her to the meadow and stretched out our hands for the ring-around-a-rosy dance.

"No, no," Aunt Isabell said. "First we must make wreaths for our hair." We all did except Nurse Amelia. She sat down and watched.

And then we danced. Aunt Isabell started a song, Nurse Amelia sang second voice and we blended in for the repeat at the end of each verse. It was a funny song and we often interrupted our singing to laugh.

Aunt Isabell was happy. We could all see and feel it, and we were happy too.

But suddenly the bushes rustled, the branches parted and there stood Magda. She was very close to us.

Aunt Isabell stopped singing and dancing and, for a few seconds, just stared at her. Then Magda made a step toward Aunt Isabell and Aunt Isabell rushed forward and hit Magda with such an impact that she fell down. Aunt Isabell was on top of Magda, hammering with her fists on Magda's chest. Magda screamed, but Aunt Isabell screamed louder.

"You monster! You sharp-fanged monster! You live here in the bushes. It was *you* who killed my bridegroom!"

Instantly Nurse Amelia was on her feet and beside the wrestling couple. With great effort she separated them.

Still screaming, Magda disappeared into the bushes.

"Free, free, free," Aunt Isabell cried. She reached for our hands and started singing again, resuming the song at exactly the point where she had been interrupted a few moments before. We were quite frightened.

Nurse Amelia stood with a frozen smile on her face. After a moment she suggested we all go back to the house.

"Not enough dancing, not enough dancing," Aunt Isabell lamented.

But Nurse Amelia took a firm grip on one of Aunt Isabell's arms and asked me to take the other.

Aunt Isabell did not resist much. She just kept on murmuring, "Not enough dancing."

* * *

Dodo was surprised to see us back so soon. We would not have told her anything, but, of course, Nurse Amelia had to. Mother ran to the telephone immediately to talk to Magda's mother. She apologized again and again. It even sounded as if she were ashamed. "My poor, poor sister," she said, now close to tears. "She is so sick. So sick."

We could not hear what Magda's mother said, but Erika whispered furiously, "Stupid Magda! It was all her fault. I had *told* her to stay out of sight!"

* * *

Before bedtime Erika and I took a walk through our garden. Magda seemed to be waiting for us and motioned us to the fence at a spot where the forsythia thinned a bit. This was where we usually

had our fence chats. We could see at once Magda was angry.

"You should have told me your Aunt Isabell was not only crazy but mean," she hissed. "Mean, mean, mean! I have never seen such a mean person."

"No," I said, "she is not mean."

And Erika said, "If you had not come out of the bushes, poor Aunt Isabell would not have become so frightened."

"I don't frighten anybody," Magda said sulkily. "I'm a good girl."

"Yes, yes, you are," I said, "but Aunt Isabell was startled. You see, she sometimes *thinks* she sees things that don't exist."

"Crazy," Magda said, "crazy as a loon."

Erika turned her back on Magda and left.

"Good night, Magda," I said and followed Erika.

Chapter Five

As I entered the dining room early the next morning, Dodo was setting the table for breakfast.

"Dodo," I asked timidly, "is Aunt Isabell as crazy as a loon?"

"No, darling, Aunt Isabell is sick."

"But they say she is crazy."

"Who is *they*?" Dodo wanted to know.

"Well...Magda."

Dodo's face got very sad. "Aunt Isabell's mind is sick," she said, "and, as with all sicknesses, there is hope it will get well again."

I wanted to ask more questions, but the door was

pushed open. Red-faced and excited, Nurse Amelia entered.

"Is Miss Isabell here?" she asked.

"Of course not," Dodo answered. "She was in her room with you when I left five minutes ago."

"I know, I know, but she's not there now!"

"How is that possible?" Dodo asked in alarm.

"I must have dozed off for a few seconds," Nurse Amelia said desperately. "I had such a bad night. Miss Isabell must have taken the key from my pocket and let herself out."

Dodo stepped into the hall and called for Mother. I called for Erika. We locked up the dog Roland so he would not frighten Aunt Isabell. Then we hurried out into the garden, each of us in a different direction. We looked under all the bushes and up all the trees. We ran to the brook, crossed it and hoped to see Aunt Isabell there. We looked and we looked, but we could not find her anywhere.

"We have to search the house," Mother said. "I will start at the attic. Dodo and Nurse Amelia will begin with the cellar."

"And we will go to the railroad station!" Erika exclaimed. "She might be there."

"Good idea," Dodo said hastily and went into the house.

Erika and I ran to the station. And there, at the very spot where the three of us had been before, stood Aunt Isabell, her arms on the fence, watching for the trains. She wasn't bothering anybody and nobody bothered her.

"Aunt Isabell," I said breathlessly, "what are you doing here?"

"Watching the trains," she answered calmly. Then she saw the perspiration on our foreheads, took her handkerchief out of her pocket and wiped our brows. "What are you so excited about?" she asked.

Erika pulled herself together first. "We *missed* you, Aunt Isabell. We all missed you."

"Nobody misses me." Aunt Isabell sighed. "All they do is *watch* me. Just watch me. They would like to put a chain around my neck. Only with you two can I dance and sing and go for walks. Everybody else locks me up—in that room upstairs."

Neither Erika nor I knew what to say. We reached for Aunt Isabell's hands and stood with her. An express train came roaring past at a tremendous speed.

"This one might be going to Paris," Aunt Isabell said. "That's where the real life is—Paris. All night long girls dance half naked in the Moulin Rouge.

Couples, kissing each other, stroll along the avenues till long past midnight, and the Eiffel Tower shoots up high in the sky and sparkles. Everybody is so gay. Only once in a while..." she added after a little pause, "once in a while someone climbs the Eiffel Tower to its uppermost deck and then—jumps off."

Aunt Isabell looked at our frightened faces.

"Sometimes," she repeated, "only sometimes."

"Let's go home now, Aunt Isabell, *please,*" I begged.

"Yes, *please,*" Erika repeated. "We haven't had breakfast yet."

"Of course, of course," Aunt Isabell replied, "if you are hungry, we must go home now. But one day I will take you to Paris."

On the way home she started to sing. This time she sang in French so we could not join her. But she sounded happy and content.

When we arrived home, Aunt Isabell was led up to her room immediately. She had stopped singing and halfway up the stairs she turned her head to us and said, "You see?"

Chapter Six

From then on they kept an even tighter watch on Aunt Isabell. A cot was put in the hall by the door to her room. Dodo and Nurse Amelia took turns sleeping there while the other was with Aunt Isabell inside her room.

We had no chance to see Aunt Isabell for many days. We would have liked to talk to her and have her tell us more about Paris, where people danced and kissed all night in the streets and sometimes jumped off the Eiffel Tower. But Aunt Isabell was kept locked up.

Erika and I talked about her often while we sat in

the shade at the brook during the long, hot summer days.

"Why are you crying?" Erika asked, seeing a tear roll down my cheek.

"A *chain* around her neck" was all I could whisper.

Just then we heard Mother's voice, loud and excited, calling us from the house.

"Come—come quickly!"

We were at her side in no time.

"She's done it *again*," Mother said. "She's gone! You two run to the railroad station!"

Off we ran. Breathless, we arrived at the station. No Aunt Isabell. Erika went to the ticket window and asked the man if he had seen the lady we had been at the station with before.

"Oh, the crazy one," he said. "No, haven't seen her today."

We ran back home. It was hard to look at the disappointed faces of Dodo, Mother and Nurse Amelia. They, too, had not found Aunt Isabell.

"I must call the police again," Mother said. She did, and she informed us they would send out one man on a search immediately and a second one would be at our house soon.

He arrived promptly. He had a dog with him who,

he said, could pick up a trail. He started at Aunt Isabell's room and let the dog sniff Aunt Isabell's bed for several minutes. Then the dog, nose close to the ground, started to move slowly out the door, down the stairs to the ground floor. He stopped at the cellar door and barked.

"She can't be in the basement," Mother said. "We searched every corner down there."

But the policeman said, "Let's follow the dog."

We all trailed behind him. The dog crossed the large basement twice. Then he sniffed at several small alcoves until he stopped and barked at the ceiling.

"Oh, yes," Dodo said, "there is this old trapdoor used years ago to get coal and firewood down to the basement."

It was not hard to push it open, and walking up a slanting board we were out in the bright daylight. Then the dog went straight to a cluster of bushes.

"We have looked there," Erika said. And we had. But we had not noticed the round wooden plank, overgrown with foliage, that covered a cement cistern. The cistern held water coming from a spring before it was pumped into the house. The dog circled the cistern and barked. The policeman took a small axlike tool and chopped away branches so we could follow the dog. Then he pushed off the wooden cover, pointed his flashlight down the shaft and heaved a big sigh. We all bent over and looked down. There was Aunt Isabell's head just above the surface of the water. She raised her head and her eyes wandered from one face to the other. She did not say a word.

"Give me your hands," the policeman said, bending down deep. But Aunt Isabell did not move. Only her eyes kept moving, searching our eyes.

I started to weep.

"Don't," Erika whispered, "don't be a crybaby now."

"Someone go and fetch a ladder," the policeman ordered, and Mother and I went to get one.

"My God," Mother moaned all the way to the house. "Oh, my God, my God."

And I let my tears run.

As soon as we were back with the ladder, the policeman lowered it into the water and started to climb down. But he soon found out the shaft was too narrow for him to climb in *and* carry up Aunt Isabell.

"We must coax her out," he said.

Dodo talked first to Aunt Isabell, but she did not respond at all. She did not even look up at us. All we

could see was the top of her head—motionless. Then Mother tried.

"Isabell, my dear, dear sister," she sobbed. She stopped a moment, controlled herself and spoke clearly. "Isabell, come up the ladder. *Please* come. It must be cold down there."

Aunt Isabell did not move or answer. Nurse Amelia tried next and so did the policeman again. All in vain.

Finally I swung my legs over the cistern's rim, got on the ladder and stepped down as far as I could. I crouched on the rung directly above Aunt Isabell and touched her head with my hand. By bending down a bit farther I could put my mouth close to her ear.

"You *can't* stay here, Aunt Isabell," I whispered. "You promised to take us to Paris one day, remember?"

She raised her head and looked at me.

"Yes, I did," she answered and smiled. "Good you reminded me—because promises must be kept."

"Let's climb out now," I said, and willingly Aunt Isabell followed me up the ladder.

Dodo had sent Nurse Amelia to the house for a huge towel. She wrapped the towel around Aunt

Isabell and led her back to her room. We all followed.

And again Aunt Isabell turned her head back at mid-stair, searched for my eyes and said, "You see?"

Chapter Seven

A terrible night followed. There was a steady coming and going, and we, though forbidden to leave our beds, could not sleep. The doctor came, and as he passed our bedroom on the way out, we could hear him say to Father, "I'll have the ambulance here tomorrow around noon. I hope she will sleep till then and the fever will be down a few degrees."

The front door closed behind him. We heard Dodo weep. Mother was sobbing too, trying to console Dodo. Then I began to cry and the next thing I felt was Erika's warm body slip into my bed and under the cover.

"Don't you cry, my little one," she whispered.

But I could hardly understand her because she was crying too.

* * *

We must have fallen asleep in each other's arms. That's how we woke next morning with Dodo's face bent over us.

"It's long past breakfast time," she said, trying to smile.

We got up and dressed. It was past ten o'clock. We nibbled at the bread and jam left out for us on the table. Neither Mother nor Dodo joined us. There was a lot of commotion upstairs, and nobody paid any attention to us.

We went into the hall, hoping to meet Dodo. When she finally came downstairs carrying a suitcase, we asked whether we could go up and see Aunt Isabell.

"No," she answered, "she is still asleep. The doctor gave her a heavy dose of morphine."

She put her suitcase close to the front door and quickly went upstairs again.

"Morphine!" I said and looked at Erika. "That has a scary sound."

"Yes." Erika nodded. "It has. And as far as I know

only sick people, *terribly* sick people, get it."

We stood around in the hall, but we seemed to be in everybody's way. Nurse Amelia nearly knocked me down carrying her own two suitcases to the entrance door.

"Why don't you two go outside?" she asked. It sounded more like an order than a question.

So we did, but we stayed close to the house. We sat down in the vine-covered gazebo in the front flower garden.

"Everything looks so pretty," Erika said after a while.

"Yes, and peaceful, too," I added. "Nobody passing could tell what an unhappy house and garden this is right now."

At that moment a big car marked *ambulance* came to a halt at our garden gate. The doctor jumped out quickly and behind him two young men in white. They lifted a strange thing out of the car—a long white canvas, stretched between two metal rods. They all walked toward the house quickly. Mother opened the door and let them in.

"Be careful with that stretcher," the doctor said.

Then nothing happened for a long time. We just sat there, keeping our eyes fixed on the main door.

Finally the door opened. First Nurse Amelia

appeared carrying her two big suitcases, which seemed no effort at all for her huge body. Then the doctor came out, now walking slowly, his head turned back to watch the two, white-dressed young men. They, too, walked slowly, carrying the stretcher between them. Dodo and Mother followed. Mother had a handkerchief pressed to her mouth and her head was bent low. Dodo walked straight as always, but her face, in the shadow of her hat, we could not see.

It took us a few seconds to realize there was a body on the stretcher, a body, covered with a white sheet, tied down by wide belts. Three of them! Erika gripped my hands.

"Aunt Isabell," she whispered. "It must be Aunt Isabell!"

I knew she was right and I started to tremble.

The long procession moved slowly along the flower-bordered path to the gate where the ambulance was parked. Leaving the garden, they were out of our sight. We heard shuffling and hushed voices. Then Dodo's voice came from inside the ambulance. She was talking to Mother. "I'll be back as soon as possible, but don't expect me before tomorrow."

The door of the ambulance was shut. The motor was started.

"Is she dead?" I asked Erika.

Erika could not speak. She shrugged her shoulders.

"And I never told her I loved her," I whispered through my tears.

At that moment the motor was shut off again and Mother called.

"Erika! Inge! Where are you? Come here. Come quickly!"

We went to the garden gate.

"Come, come," Mother urged us. "Aunt Isabell is awake now and she wants to say good-bye to you."

We climbed into the ambulance and stood beside Aunt Isabell. She, still strapped down under the white sheet, turned her head to us. She saw our red, teary eyes and smiled.

"Don't cry," she said slowly and tenderly. "I know you love me. You don't have to prove it with tears."

She paused, then continued. "I guess you know I am sick. Very sick. Though *one day* I will be fine again and I will be back. And then...you know what?...Then the three of us will go to Paris. I promised you, remember?"

She smiled encouragingly, tried to raise herself, but could not. Still smiling she closed her eyes.

"Leave now," the doctor said. "She will go back to sleep. That's the best for her."

I wanted to bend down and kiss her, but the doctor put his hands on our shoulders and made us leave.

Once more I turned back to look at her. Aunt Isabell, too, had turned her face toward us and after a last and very faint smile she pursed her lips to throw two little kisses at Erika and me.